DATE			

Yossi Asks the Angels for Help

A CHARLOTTE ZOLOTOW BOOK

Miriam Chaikin

Yossi Asks the Angels for Help

pictures by Petra Mathers

HARPER & ROW, PUBLISHERS

Yossi Asks the Angels for Help
Text copyright © 1985 by Miriam Chaikin
Illustrations copyright © 1985 by Petra Mathers
All rights reserved. No part of this book may be
used or reproduced in any manner whatsoever without
written permission except in the case of brief quotations
embodied in critical articles and reviews. Printed in
the United States of America. For information address
Harper & Row Junior Books, 10 East 53rd Street,
New York, N.Y. 10022. Published simultaneously in
Canada by Fitzhenry & Whiteside Limited, Toronto.

Library of Congress Cataloging in Publication Data
Chaikin, Miriam.
    Yossi asks the angels for help.

    Summary: When he loses the Hanukkah money he planned
to use for presents for his sister and parents, Yossi
prays to the angels for help.
    1. Children's stories, American.   [1. Hanukkah—
Fiction.   2. Jews—Fiction]   I. Mathers, Petra, ill.
II. Title.
PZ7.C3487Yo 1985   [Fic]   84-48351
ISBN 0-06-021195-4
ISBN 0-06-021196-2 (lib. bdg.)

Designed by Barbara A. Fitzsimmons
1 2 3 4 5 6 7 8 9 10
First Edition

I THOUGHT THE FIRST MOLLY BOOK WAS *IT*.
CHARLOTTE SAID THERE WAS MORE.
For Charlotte Zolotow.

Yossi Asks
the Angels
for Help

Jelly Beans

"Yossi!" the rebbe called.

Yossi nearly fell out of his chair. How come the rebbe was calling him again? He had just called on him. Yossi had only just sat down. Two seconds ago. He rose to his feet.

"Do you know the answer?" the rebbe asked.

Yossi had not heard the question. He hadn't been listening. As he had taken his seat, he had

1

closed his ears to the rebbe's voice. Sometimes he was able to cover up his inattention by fooling around. He tried it now.

"Maybe I know the answer," he said. "But a plane or something flew by when you spoke, and I didn't hear the question."

He saw his friends Zalman and Menachem Mendl cover their mouths to keep from laughing.

The rebbe tugged at his beard. "That's very strange," he said. "I didn't hear a thing."

"You were talking, probably that's why," Yossi said.

Yossi heard grunts and coughs escaping from his classmates.

The rebbe got up. He folded his hands behind himself and walked up the aisle with his back to Yossi. Yossi could tell the rebbe was getting ready to lay a trap for him.

"Let us approach the matter somewhat differently," the rebbe said. "I will give the answer, Yossi. And you must tell me what the question was."

"Oh, boy!" Yossi heard his classmates exclaim.

"The answer," the rebbe said, "is Moses." He

2

turned to face Yossi. "What was the question?"

Yossi squirmed. The rebbe wasn't being fair. Moses was known for many things. The question could be: *Which Biblical figure was born in Egypt? Or, Who freed the Jewish slaves? Or, Who received the Ten Commandments on Mount Sinai?* Yossi didn't know what to say.

"Eh-eh-eh . . ." he said, *fumf*ing.

"Well . . . ?" the rebbe said.

"It could be anything," Yossi said.

"Go to the board, Yossi," the rebbe said.

Yossi was glad to move from the spot. As he hurried forward he heard *pik, pik, pik,* a sound like single pebbles falling on a wooden floor. He didn't know what the sound was. And he didn't know why the boys started laughing. Yossi picked up a piece of chalk and turned to the rebbe.

Pik.

The boys again broke out in laughter. Yossi felt the sound was somehow related to him, but he didn't know in what way. The rebbe stood in the aisle, shaking his head. Yossi didn't know where to look.

Puk. This time Yossi felt something land on

his shoe and glanced down. A jelly bean! The jelly beans in his pocket had worn a hole through the material.

Yossi turned beet-red.

"Empty your pockets on the table, or the jelly bean concert will go on forever," the rebbe said.

Yossi removed the rest of the jelly beans from his pocket. They were melting and faded, and he was afraid to put them on the desk. He turned to say so, but the rebbe did not give him the chance.

"On the desk!" the rebbe repeated.

Yossi put the jelly beans on the desk and wiped his hand on the blackboard eraser.

"Write as follows," the rebbe said.

Chalk in hand, Yossi turned to the board.

"Moses and the Maccabees won a victory over Israel's oppressors, and that is why we celebrate the holiday of Hanukkah."

Yossi spun around. Had the rebbe gone bonkers? The eight-day holiday of Hanukkah started tonight. The Maccabees had won the victory. Moses had nothing to do with Hanukkah. He wasn't even alive then.

"But Moses wasn't—"

"Write!" the rebbe said.

Yossi wrote the sentence out on the board then turned to face the rebbe.

"Class," the rebbe said. "Do you see what is written on the board?"

"We see," the boys answered in a chorus.

The rebbe looked at Yossi. "Would you say that what you have written is the statement of a smart person?"

Yossi shook his head.

"It's the statement of—what kind of person?" the rebbe asked.

Yossi hesitated. If he said *stupid*, the rebbe might think Yossi was calling him names. After all, it was the rebbe's sentence.

"I'm waiting," the rebbe said.

"S-stupid?" Yossi said gingerly.

The class laughed.

"Ignorant is a better word," the rebbe said. "It means uneducated. If you don't pay attention in class, you'll go through life saying stupid things like that."

Yossi laughed along with the boys.

"Return to your seat," the rebbe said. "And pick up the jelly beans."

Yossi started to take the jelly beans from the desk.

"Not those, from the floor," the rebbe said.

Yossi picked up the jelly beans, threw them into the wastebasket at the side of the rebbe's desk, and sat down.

The rebbe also returned to his seat. He opened a book on his desk and stroked his beard, preparing a discussion.

"Two boys were walking down the street," he said in his example-giving voice. "At the same moment they both spotted a dollar on the sidewalk. We don't know whose dollar it was. Somebody lost it. One boy falls on the dollar saying, 'It's mine!' The other boy pulls the dollar out from under him and says, 'It's mine! Here it is, in my hand.' "

The rebbe looked up. "To whom does the dollar belong?"

Zalman raised his hand.

"The first boy owns it because he fell on it and covered it with his body," he said.

7

"What's the big deal?" the rebbe said. "If he fell on an automobile, or an apartment house, and said it was his, would that make it his?"

Avram Lev, the class showoff, rose. "It's the second boy's dollar because he had it in his hand. That made it his."

The rebbe nodded. "Possession usually makes it his."

Yossi wondered if he could get back his jelly beans. They might be sticky and faded, but they were still good. He raised his hand.

"Yossi," the rebbe said.

Yossi rose. "Everybody knows the jelly beans are mine. But right now, they're on your desk. I think I still own them."

The rebbe made a face at the jelly beans and the boys laughed. With the side of his hand, he swept the jelly beans from the desk, into the waiting basket below.

"The wastebasket owns the jelly beans," he said.

Yossi sat down. He thought it was mean of the rebbe to do that. Good jelly beans, wasted. Yossi did not raise his hand the whole afternoon, even if he knew an answer, to spite the rebbe.

The rebbe closed his book. He glanced around the class. "I'm letting you go home early today," he said.

"Yay!" the boys yelled.

Yossi's high spirits returned at once.

"Does anyone know why I'm letting you go home early?" the rebbe asked.

"Because it's the first night of Hanukkah," someone called.

"Anything else?"

"Because we light the first candle tonight," Avram Lev said.

"I'm letting you go home early because I want you to be able to rest before you light the candle. Who knows why?"

Yossi and the other boys exchanged puzzled glances.

"Because I want you to have enough strength to strike the match," the rebbe said.

"Ooh— Ugh!" Yossi and the boys half groaned, half laughed at the rebbe's joke.

9

"So. . . . Happy Hanukkah!" the rebbe called.

Everyone jumped up. Yossi sat near the door and was out before Zalman and Menachem Mendl. He waited on the stoop for his friends to come out. They lived on the same block and walked home with him.

Empty Pockets

Yossi thought excitedly about the evening. Normally, he would have received his Hanukkah *gelt*, the money gift that was given on the holiday, after supper. But the money was already in his pocket. He had told his parents he needed it early, to buy Rivkaleh, his little sister, the ring in the five-and-ten she wanted. She knew he was getting it for her. But his parents did not know that he planned to buy each of them a present too.

"Listen," he said as Zalman and Menachem Mendl came through the door. "I have to go to the five-and-ten to buy presents. It'll only take a second. I know what I want. Come with me."

"Sure," Zalman said. "It's early. My mother isn't expecting me yet."

Menachem Mendl nodded okay. "Do you give presents for Hanukkah in your house?" he asked as they all went down the steps together.

"Usually no," Yossi said. "But this year, I'm doing something different. I'm using my Hanukkah money to buy presents for my family."

"In my house, it's the same every year," Zalman said. "Every day I get ten cents Hanukkah *gelt*. My sister gets five. And the baby gets a penny to put in the charity box for Israel."

Yossi said nothing about how much he had, but he felt like a millionaire. His parents had given him two dollars this year.

"My parents can't afford Hanukkah *gelt*," Menachem Mendl said. "There are too many of us. We each get little bags with nuts and raisins. But I'm doing something different this year too. I'm giving everyone a present."

"Where are you getting the money?" Yossi asked.

"It's not costing me a cent," Menachem Mendl said.

"How come?" Zalman asked.

"I'm giving them myself."

Yossi and Zalman stopped to look at him. "Yourself?"

"Why not?" Menachem Mendl said. "A present doesn't have to come from a store. I'm the present. Each one can have me for an hour. I'll be a robot, and do whatever they want. Play games. Do favors. Whatever they want."

"That's a great idea," Yossi said. "Maybe next year I'll do that too. But this year, I promised my sister a ring." He smiled. "I'm getting presents for my parents too, but they don't know. It's a surprise. I told Rivkaleh, but she'll keep the secret."

At the five-and-ten, Yossi had a shock. When he put his hand in his pocket for money, he found his pocket empty.

The boys looked at him.

"What's the matter?"

"Did you lose something?"

"I put eight quarters in my pocket this morning," Yossi said. "But now it's empty."

"Well, if the left side of the pants is as old as the right side," Zalman said, "probably the same thing that happened to the jelly beans happened to the quarters."

"But there was no hole in my pocket when I left the house," Yossi said.

"If jelly beans can make a hole, what do you think quarters can do?" Menachem Mendl said.

Yossi felt again in his pocket as the boys watched in silence. He pulled the pocket up and stared at the hole in the seam. "I never heard them fall," he said, mystified.

Zalman and Menachem Mendl smiled at each other.

"With you, it's not a surprise," Zalman said.

"Let's face it, Yossi," Menachem Mendl said. "You don't pay attention. That's why you get into trouble at school."

"Look who's talking," Yossi said.

"So what will you do?" Zalman asked.

"Kill myself," Yossi said.

"Besides that?"

Yossi shrugged. "Where am I going to get two dollars?"

"I'll get my first ten cents tonight," Zalman said. "I can lend it to you, if you want."

Yossi shook his head. Ten cents was too little. Besides, Zalman hadn't sounded too eager.

"We might as well go," Yossi said, dejected.

The boys walked home in silence.

"I have an idea," Zalman said suddenly. "Tell your mother and father you were going to surprise them. They'll be just as glad. Then you'll only have half a problem."

"Yeah," Yossi said. "The hard part, my little sister."

"I know what," Menachem Mendl said. "Tell her instead of giving it to her on the first night of Hanukkah, you'll give it to her tomorrow, on the second night."

"Where is the money supposed to come from tomorrow?" Yossi asked.

"Pray for a miracle," Menachem Mendl said.

16

When they reached Yossi's house, they saw Rivkaleh looking out the window.

"There she is . . ." Yossi said.

"Look," Menachem Mendl said. "They say angels come on Friday night, when we light Sabbath candles, right?"

Yossi nodded.

"Maybe angels come when we light Hanukkah candles too."

Yossi had never heard of that.

"Good luck," Zalman said and walked away.

"*Gut yonteff*, happy holiday," Menachem Mendl said.

"Same to you," Yossi answered in a small voice.

As Yossi went up the steps of the stoop he saw Rivkaleh leave the window. He knew she would be waiting for him in the vestibule of the apartment. He stood for a moment collecting his thoughts.

Menachem Mendl might have been kidding. But what if he was right? After all, everyone thought angels came on Friday night. There was even a song about it. Why couldn't they come on Hanukkah too? Maybe they did, and nobody ever noticed it. Maybe he would be the first to discover it.

The idea cheered him. Angels were God's helpers. They could make miracles. He looked up at the sky.

"Holy One," he said, "I hate to bother you, but I'm in a pickle. I had money to buy presents for everyone for Hanukkah, and I lost it. The main thing is, I hate to disappoint my little sister. If angels do come on Hanukkah, please tell them to see me. I need help."

Company for Supper

Yossi felt terrible, watching the look of excitement on Rivkaleh's face change to gloom.

"Guess what?" he said, forcing his voice to sound cheerful.

Rivkaleh regarded him in silence.

"I just came from the five-and-ten. They had one ruby ring left, but it was broken, so I didn't

buy it. The saleslady said she would have another one for me tomorrow."

Rivkaleh looked as if she were about to cry. "The presents for Mama and Papa, were they broken too?"

Yossi had forgotten to take that into account. "Shhh," he said, putting a finger to his lips. "It's a secret."

"I know it's a secret," Rivkaleh said with a trembly chin.

"I—I figured I'd get everything tomorrow, all at the same time."

Rivkaleh glanced away.

"It's only one more day," Yossi said.

"It was supposed to be tonight, on the *first* night of Hanukkah."

"So it'll be on the second night. It's not so terrible. Wait till you see how pretty it is," Yossi added, trying to make her feel better.

"Is that you, Yossi?" Mama called from the kitchen.

"It's me," Yossi sang back. He put down his schoolbag. On the way to the kitchen he noticed

21

the *hanukkiah*, the nine-cup candlestick used on Hanukkah, in the living room, and went to look at it. He saw Rivkaleh hurry into the kitchen to complain about him.

Yossi looked at the two candles Mama had placed in their cups, and the matches nearby. "Even unlit," he thought, "the candles give the room a holiday look." He gave the candlestick a friendly tap, wondering if he would see angels dancing when the candles were lit.

"If only . . ." he thought, going into the kitchen.

Mama was at the stove. Rivkaleh was beside her, wearing a sour face.

"Hi, Mama. The kitchen looks nice," he said.

The table was covered with a pretty cloth, and arranged for six people, two more than usual. Papa was bringing home two guests, the boy who worked in his store and the boy's girl friend.

"Yossi," Mama said. "The jelly beans were supposed to last for the whole holiday. Already, an inch is missing."

Yossi felt guilty. He was not supposed to take cake or candy without permission.

22

"I took a few, Ma, but it was no inch."

To his relief, the door clicked open, bringing the conversation to a close.

"Papa!" Rivkaleh cried, running to greet him.

Yossi saw Papa give her a *dreidl*, a toy top used for playing Hanukkah games.

Papa came into the kitchen with Rivkaleh in his arms and the guests following. He introduced them.

"Meet Steven, and his fiancée, Julie," he said. "And this is my wife, and my son, Yossi."

"Come in, come in," Mama said. "Steven, I hear so much about you. It's nice to meet you finally." She turned to the girl. "It's nice to meet you too, Julie."

Yossi was glad the company had come. They were making a fuss over Rivkaleh, and his little sister had found other things to think about for the moment. He glanced into the living room. "Angels," he said to himself, "please come." But the angels wouldn't come until the candles were lit. Yossi was impatient for the lighting ceremony.

23

"Why are we all standing in the kitchen?" he said, to hurry things along. "Why don't we go in the living room, and light the candles?"

Mama gave him a questioning glance.

"We light candles when it gets dark," Papa said. "It's not yet dark. Another few minutes." He turned toward the living room. "But come, Yossi is right," he said. "It's more comfortable in there."

Yossi went to stand near the candlestick, thinking that might make time move more quickly. Everyone took seats. Mama came in with a dish of olives and Yossi ran to take one; but she moved the dish out of his reach and offered it first to Julie, then to Steven. When everyone had taken olives she put the dish on the table and sat down next to Rivkaleh on the couch.

Papa looked at Yossi. "Why are you standing there, like a street light?" he said. "Sit down."

Yossi shuffled over to a chair. He sat at the edge and turned so he could see the window. The night was growing darker—but not fast enough.

"What's a feensay, Papa?" Rivkaleh asked.

"Where did you hear such a word?" Papa said, putting his olive pit into a dish.

24

"I bet she means *fiancée*," Julie said.

"Oh, fiancée?" Papa said. "That means that Julie and Steven will soon be getting married."

"When will I get married?" Rivkaleh asked.

"Is there someone you'd like to marry?" Mama asked.

"I want to marry Papa."

Yossi gave his sister a look of disgust. "Dopey," he said. "You can't marry your own father."

"Then I'll marry you."

Yossi popped an olive into his mouth and licked his fingers. "You can't marry me either, I'm your brother," he said. "You can't marry anyone in your own family."

Rivkaleh began to cry.

"Rivkaleh," Mama said, taking the little girl onto her lap. "What is it?"

"I don't want to marry a stranger," Rivkaleh said.

Yossi and everyone watched as Mama rocked Rivkaleh to soothe her.

"Rivkaleh," Mama said. "You won't have to marry a stranger."

Rivkaleh looked up.

"You'll marry someone you know very, very well. I promise," Mama said.

Rivkaleh blinked her tears back and slid over onto her own seat.

Yossi turned back to the window.

"I see it's getting dark," he said.

"Almost," Papa said.

Yossi detected a note of annoyance in his father's voice.

"Actually," Steven said, "we're not getting married too soon. We both want to finish college first."

Yossi spun around. If Steven went to college, he had to be smart. Yossi was about to ask him if he had any ideas about how to raise two dollars in a hurry, but decided against it. He had already asked the angels for help. If he asked Steven too, the angels might get insulted and stay away. He looked out the window.

"Look how dark it's getting," he said.

The little vein that stood out in Papa's forehead when he got angry stood out. "Yossi, what's the matter with you? You know very well that for candle lighting, it's dark when three stars appear in the sky. And not before."

Yossi could hardly stand the waiting. But he did not want to annoy his father, either. He sat down on the edge of the chair again and forced himself to follow the conversation as Steven and Julie asked questions about Hanukkah. It amazed him that they were Jews and didn't know anything about their own holiday.

Papa told how two thousand years ago the conquerors of Jerusalem tried to force the Jews to stop being Jews, and how the Maccabees, the Jewish rebels, fought back.

"So tonight, we celebrate the victory of the Maccabees," Papa said.

"But you said it was an eight-day holiday," Julie said. "Where do the eight days come in?"

Yossi gave a look of disgust. "A couple of dummies," he thought. "Even Rivkaleh knows more."

"The conquerors ruined the Temple," Papa explained. "The Jews cleaned it, and wanted to light the menorah—"

"That's a candlestick," Yossi offered. "Only they burned oil, not candles, in those days."

Papa nodded. "Somebody found a vial of oil that was enough to last for one day. By some miracle, it lasted for eight days."

The word miracle stirred Yossi.

"Rivkaleh, go see if there are three stars in the sky yet," he said, knowing she wouldn't be blamed for anything.

Rivkaleh dutifully went to the window and looked out. "I can't see, it's too dark," she said.

Papa rose. "It's time," he said. "We can light the candles now."

Yossi knocked over his chair in his rush to get up.

Mama gave him a look.

"Yossi!" Papa said.

The Candles Are Lit

Papa gave Steven a skull cap to put on, and everyone gathered around the *hanukkiah*.

"Children," Papa said, "since Steven and Julie have never lit candles before, I think we should let them say the blessings for all of us tonight. Do you agree?"

Yossi liked to light the candles himself. But he

would have agreed to anything to see the candles lit. "Sure," he said.

"Let Steven do it alone," Julie said shyly.

"I'll be glad to, but I don't read Hebrew," Steven said.

Papa brought a book from the bookcase and opened it to the right page. "Here are the blessings in English," he said.

Steven smiled at Julie, then looked at the words, preparing himself.

"You light the top candle first," Yossi said, speaking quickly. "That candle is like a torch. You use it to light the other one."

"I see. . . ." Steven said.

"You're doing a good job of explaining, Yossi," Papa said.

Yossi didn't want to say his only interest was in getting started.

"Tell about my part, Mama," Rivkaleh said.

"After Steven says the blessings, Rivkaleh will sing a song for us," Mama said.

Yossi winced. He had heard Mama teaching Rivkaleh the song. Rivkaleh kept starting and stopping and couldn't remember the words. He picked up the matches. "Here," he said, handing them to Steven.

Steven lit the candles. They glowed and twinkled. The room seemed brighter to Yossi. Could it be that the angels had come? He squinted, peering around the flames, while beside him Steven recited the blessings.

"Blessed is God, king of the universe,
who has given us laws to live by and
commanded us to light candles for Hanukkah.

"Blessed is God, king of the universe,
who performed miracles for our ancestors
in days gone by, at this time.

"Blessed is God, king of the universe,
who has kept us in health and allowed
us to reach this season."

Try as he might, Yossi couldn't see a thing. But he thought he heard something, a kind of soft whispering.

"Now comes my part," Rivkaleh said.

"Wait a minute," Yossi said, trying to catch the tiny sound.

"Ma, he's not going to let me sing," Rivkaleh said.

"Of course he'll let you," Mama said. She gave Yossi a stern look. "What are you doing, anyhow?"

"Someone said angels come when Hanukkah candles are lit," he said. "I was just trying to see if he was right."

"There are angels every day," Papa said, "but we can't see them." He then looked at Yossi suspiciously. "Why are you looking for angels? Are you in trouble at school again?"

"No," Yossi said with a big smile, to show how free he was of trouble. "I was just wondering if the guy was right." He turned to Rivkaleh. "Let's hear Rivkaleh sing her song," he said, to change the subject.

"Yes, let's," Julie said.

Mama straightened Rivkaleh's collar. "Are you ready?"

Rivkaleh nodded and began, singing the Yiddish song she had been practicing all week.

"Oi ye klayneh liktelak
yeer dertselt gishiktelak
miselak fun amull,
yir dertselt fun mootikite,
beriershaft une blutikite,
nissim un a tsull."

(Little candles all aglow
telling tales of long ago,
stories that are true.
I know well the tales you tell,
of honor, glory, tears as well—
and miracles, those too.)

Yossi listened with the others to her song. For one thing, Mama was watching him. For another, it sounded a lot better than he thought it would. She had sung straight through, without stopping. Yossi clapped along with the others.

Then he took advantage of the excitement over

33

Rivkaleh to study the flames. They were even brighter than before. There had to be angels now! Nothing else could make such a sweet glow. He walked around the candlestick, bending close to see better.

"Come," Mama said. "It's time for roast chicken and potato *latkes*."

Another time Yossi would have been the first one at the table. He loved his mother's potato pancakes. But tonight, he hung back and let the others go. Mama, Papa and Rivkaleh led the way; Steven and Julie followed. Julie glanced back at Yossi. He waved, and turned back to the flames.

He was glad at last to be alone with the angels— if they were there. Now, with the others gone, he might be able to see them better. If not, he would certainly hear the whispering more clearly in the empty room.

As he scrutinized the flames he listened hard, trying to catch the whispering.

"Yossi!" Papa called.

"Are you there, angels?" Yossi asked, tiptoeing around the candlestick.

"Yossi!" Mama's voice followed. "We're waiting!"

"Angels," Yossi whispered, "I need two dollars by tomorrow. The Holy One, praised be he, knows the whole story. Get the details from him," he said, and hurried into the kitchen.

A Do-It-Yourself Miracle

The next morning, Yossi told his mother about the torn pockets, and she gave him another pair of pants to put on. As he sat at the breakfast table with Rivkaleh he thought about last night. He hadn't actually seen angels, but he had heard them. He was sure of it. If it had been quieter in the room, he would have heard their exact words. The whispering, he thought, had sounded something like—*Don't worry . . . fix everything.* By the time Yossi was through eating he had convinced himself that the angels were taking care of everything, and he had nothing to worry about.

"I'm finished," he said, getting up from the table.

Mama was at the sink. "Don't touch the jelly beans," she said.

"I won't."

"If I didn't know better, I would think they don't give you enough to eat in school."

"They don't," Yossi said. He took up his schoolbag. With a finger to his lips he signaled Rivkaleh to be quiet, and tiptoed to the cupboard. Mama had forbidden him to take jelly beans. But she hadn't said anything about cake. He broke off a piece of cake, wrapped it in a paper napkin and put it in his bag.

"So long," he said, heading for the door.

"It's the second night of Hanukkah!" Rivkaleh called from the table.

With his chin, Yossi indicated the window. "I said, *night.* So far, it's still day." He opened the door and went out.

So sure was Yossi that the angels were already

at work for him, he looked about expecting a miracle. He was sure the man walking toward him would press two dollars into his hand, and disappear. When that didn't happen, he looked up to see if perhaps an envelope was floating down from heaven. When that didn't happen, he searched the ground for a mysterious package. But nothing unusual happened on the way to school.

He waved to Zalman and Menachem Mendl as he took his seat in class. He thought it had been foolish of the angels not to help him outside. There were more opportunities for miracles in the street. They only made things harder for themselves, waiting until he got into class. He shrugged, hoping the angels knew what they were doing.

The wall clock struck eight. In the same instant, like a cuckoo sounding, the rebbe began.

"What were the Israelites doing in Egypt?" he asked.

"They were worshipping the golden calf," Menachem Mendl answered.

The rebbe gave him a look of disapproval. "That was not in Egypt, that was when they were wandering in the wilderness," he said, turning away.

"What were the Israelites doing in Egypt?" he repeated, looking at the window.

Zalman raised his hand. "They were slaves."

"*Before* they were slaves," the rebbe said, shaking a thumb backward over his shoulder to indicate the past.

Avram Lev's hand went up. "They were in Egypt because there was a famine in Canaan, in their own land," he said, "and there was plenty of food in Egypt so they went there to get food."

"Do you agree, Menachem Mendl?" the rebbe asked.

"I agree," Menachem Mendl said.

Menachem Mendl looked so serious, Yossi had to smile. As he glanced away, his eye fell on the keyhole of the door. Angels were supposed to be very tiny. He wondered if they would use the keyhole to enter.

"Yossi!"

"Yes?"

"What do you mean, yes? Do you have anything to add?"

"About what?"

41

"About the subject."

Yossi had forgotten what the subject was. He tried to recall. "About"—he almost said angels— "Egypt, you mean?"

"No, about the price of knishes on Delancey Street."

The boys laughed. Yossi shrugged. Let them laugh. What did they know about his worries?

The rebbe went on to speak about the Israelites in Egypt, and Yossi went on looking for places through which the angels might enter. When the principal came into the room, Yossi thought that would be a good time for angels to enter, but he saw none. When the rebbe opened the window with the window pole, Yossi thought surely the angels had come flying in then.

But the morning passed without angels and without miracles of any sort. Yossi decided there was only one thing for him to do—pray.

When the lunch bell rang, he went to the lunch room with Zalman and Menachem Mendl. Menachem Mendl didn't bring up angels, and neither did Yossi. He swallowed his food quickly, and told them he had to run an errand for his mother.

Outside, he passed a synagogue but did not go in. Men would be praying in there. And he wanted his prayer to rise to heaven alone, so it would have a better chance of being noticed.

Yossi walked around the block, praying.

"Holy One, I hate to bother you," he said, "but I'm in the same pickle as yesterday. I guess angels don't come on Hanukkah after all. The thing is, I still don't have money to buy Rivkaleh's present. She's only a little girl, Holy One," he added. "And she's going to be so disappointed. . . ."

"Yossi?"

Yossi looked up, startled to see the rebbe standing before him. A lit cigarette dangled from his lips, and ashes dropped down on his coat.

"I like to take a walk after lunch too," the rebbe said.

Yossi thought the rebbe had mistaken him for someone else. Why else was the rebbe talking to him as if he were a regular person?

"It's good to take a walk, huh?" the rebbe said.

"I wasn't exactly taking a walk," Yossi said.

43

"But what?" The rebbe's cigarette jiggled as he spoke.

"I was walking and praying for God's help."

A piece of cigarette paper stuck to the rebbe's lip, and he pulled it off.

"Try acting as if God doesn't exist," the rebbe said.

Yossi couldn't believe his ears. The rebbe was a teacher of religion. How could he say such a thing?

"D-doesn't exist?" Yossi sputtered.

"Right," the rebbe said. "Before you call on God, first see what you can do for yourself. That's what God wants from you."

He removed the cigarette from his lips. "See this?" he said, as if he had all along been talking about the weather.

Yossi nodded.

"This is my clock. When it goes out, I know it's time to go back to school." He tossed the stub into the gutter and walked off.

Yossi stared dumbfounded after the rebbe. *Act as if God doesn't exist.* The words had shocked him. They had been like a slap in the face. Yet, they

45

had done something. They had cleared his head. For he found himself thinking instead of wishing, thinking clear, logical thoughts.

"There was no hole in my pocket when I left the house," he said to himself. "The hole needed time to grow. That means, I didn't lose the money near the house. I didn't lose it near the school, or in class either, or one of the boys would have noticed."

Suddenly a thought, like a sharp salute, popped up in his mind.

"The grate! I bet they fell through the holes in the subway grate."

He ran the two blocks to the subway, got down on his hands and knees, and peered through the grate to the floor below. Yossi smiled. There, in plain view, was a little silver river, eight quarters strung out in a row.

It occurred to him that he was being foolish. He shouldn't be looking happy and advertising the fact that there was money down there. Someone would only come and take it while he was away at school. He got up and looked angrily at the grate, as if he had tripped over it. He walked nonchalantly to the corner. There, he began to run to school.

The rebbe was in the middle of a sentence when Yossi entered.

"Why are you late?" the rebbe asked.

"I—I acted as if there was no God," Yossi said. He smiled at the scared look that crossed Menachem Mendl's face.

"And?" the rebbe asked.

"I found what I was looking for," Yossi said, beaming.

The rebbe gave what, on his face, passed for a smile. He turned to the class. "We shouldn't bother the Holy One with every little thing," he said. "Sometimes, we must act as if there is no God, and figure things out for ourselves."

Yossi took advantage of being in the rebbe's good graces, something that rarely happened. "Rebbe, could I leave a few minutes early?" he dared to ask.

"It so happens I was planning on letting the class out early again today," the rebbe said.

As the boys let out shouts of joy, Yossi signaled

to Zalman and Menachem Mendl that he had found the money and needed their help after class.

"Silence!" the rebbe called. He tugged at his beard. "Let us return to the subject," he said.

The afternoon went quickly. Yossi had wracked his brain wondering how to get at the quarters, then realized that the window pole would be the perfect thing.

The rebbe closed his book. "All right, that's it for today," he said.

Yossi raised his hand. "Can I borrow the window pole, rebbe?" he asked.

"If you bring it back."

Yossi nodded. "Can I ask the class a question?"

"Go ahead."

Yossi faced the boys. "Does anyone have a piece of chewing gum?"

A chorus of No's went up.

"I have," the rebbe said.

"You?" Yossi asked, surprised.

"What's the matter? Is there a commandment that says a teacher is not allowed to chew gum?"

Yossi and the boys laughed.

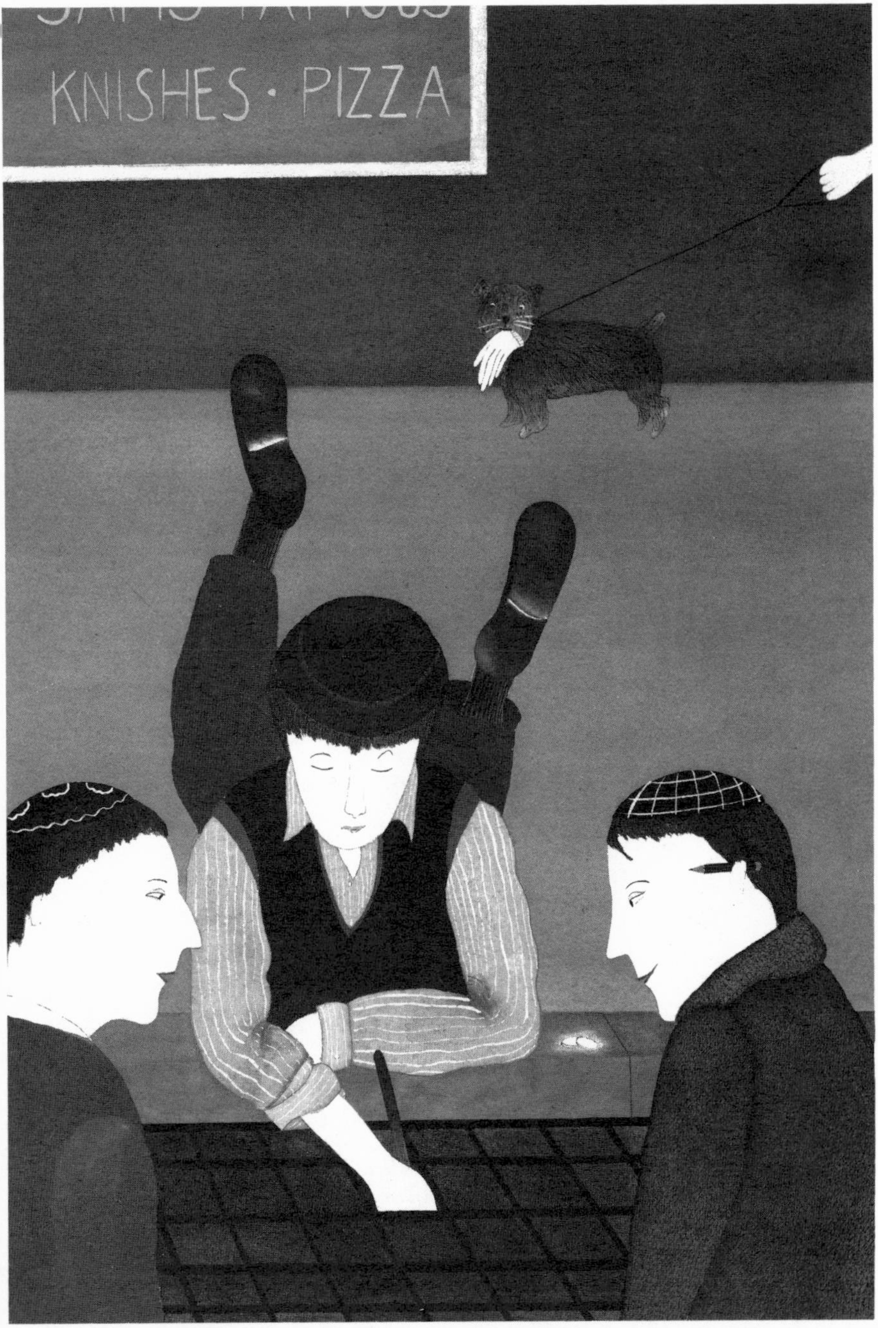
KNISHES · PIZZA

"Have a happy second night of Hanukkah," the rebbe called.

Yossi, Zalman and Menachem Mendl were soon bent over the grate. Yossi had chewed on half a piece of gum to soften it, and attached it to the pole.

"Here, you try first," he said, handing Zalman the pole. "You have the longest fingers."

Zalman looked at his hand, examining his fingers, then lowered the pole. After several tries, he brought up a quarter. After that, the boys took turns at the pole. It was not easy. Between the cold weather, freezing fingers and the heavy pole, it was hard to stab a quarter. When it started to get dark, Zalman and Menachem Mendl decided they couldn't stay any longer. Between them, they had lifted out a total of six quarters.

"Thanks a million," Yossi said. "This is great. I can buy Rivkaleh her ring, and maybe even a small present for my parents to share."

He glanced down at the remaining two quarters. "Somebody else can go after those," he said. He placed the second half-piece of gum on the

grate. "Let them also find this and think it's a miracle," he said.

The boys helped Yossi return the window pole, then went home. Yossi hurried to the five-and-ten. He bought the ruby ring, and a package of envelopes and notepaper for his mother and father. Feeling happy, he ran all the way home. He saw Rivkaleh at the window, waiting.

"I got it!" he called up, shaking the bag at her.

He knew she couldn't hear through the closed window. But his heart warmed at the look of joy on her face. He paused on the stoop and turned to look at the sky.

"Holy One," he said, "so I figured something out for myself, so what? So I took a problem off your hands, so what? It's not making me conceited. I know you put the ideas in my head, in the first place. Don't worry; with me, you'll always be boss."